Crazy about puppies?
Ready for a
heartwarming
of friendship
Want to know about real-life assistance dogs?
"A must for any children hooked on animals or school stories."
—THE TELEGRAPH
No ball games, please!

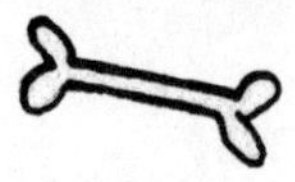

Henry Holt and Company, *Publishers since 1866*
175 Fifth Avenue, New York, New York 10010
mackids.com

Library of Congress Cataloging-in-Publication Data
Names: Lewis, Gill, author. | Horne, Sarah, 1979– illustrator.
Title: Pip and the paw of friendship / Gill Lewis ; illustrated by Sarah Horne.
Description: First American edition. | New York : Henry Holt and Company, 2017. | Series: Puppy academy | Summary: "A story about a puppy who is training to be a service dog—and the young human girl he befriends"—Provided by publisher.
Identifiers: LCCN 2016015268 (print) | LCCN 2016042640 (ebook) | ISBN 9781627797986 (hardback) | ISBN 9781250092854 (paperback) | ISBN 9781627797993 (ebook)
Subjects: | CYAC: Dogs—Training—Fiction. | Service dogs—Fiction. | Animals—Infancy—Fiction. | Human-animal relationships—Fiction. | BISAC: JUVENILE FICTION / Animals / Dogs. | JUVENILE FICTION / Action & Adventure / General. | JUVENILE FICTION / Humorous Stories.
Classification: LCC PZ7.L58537 Pi 2017 (print) | LCC PZ7.L58537 (ebook) | DDC [Fic]—dc23
LC record available at https://lccn.loc.gov/2016015268

Originally published in the UK in 2016 by Oxford University Press
First American edition—2017

Printed in the United States of America by
LSC Communications, Harrisonburg, Virginia

1 3 5 7 9 10 8 6 4 2 (hardcover)
1 3 5 7 9 10 8 6 4 2 (paperback)

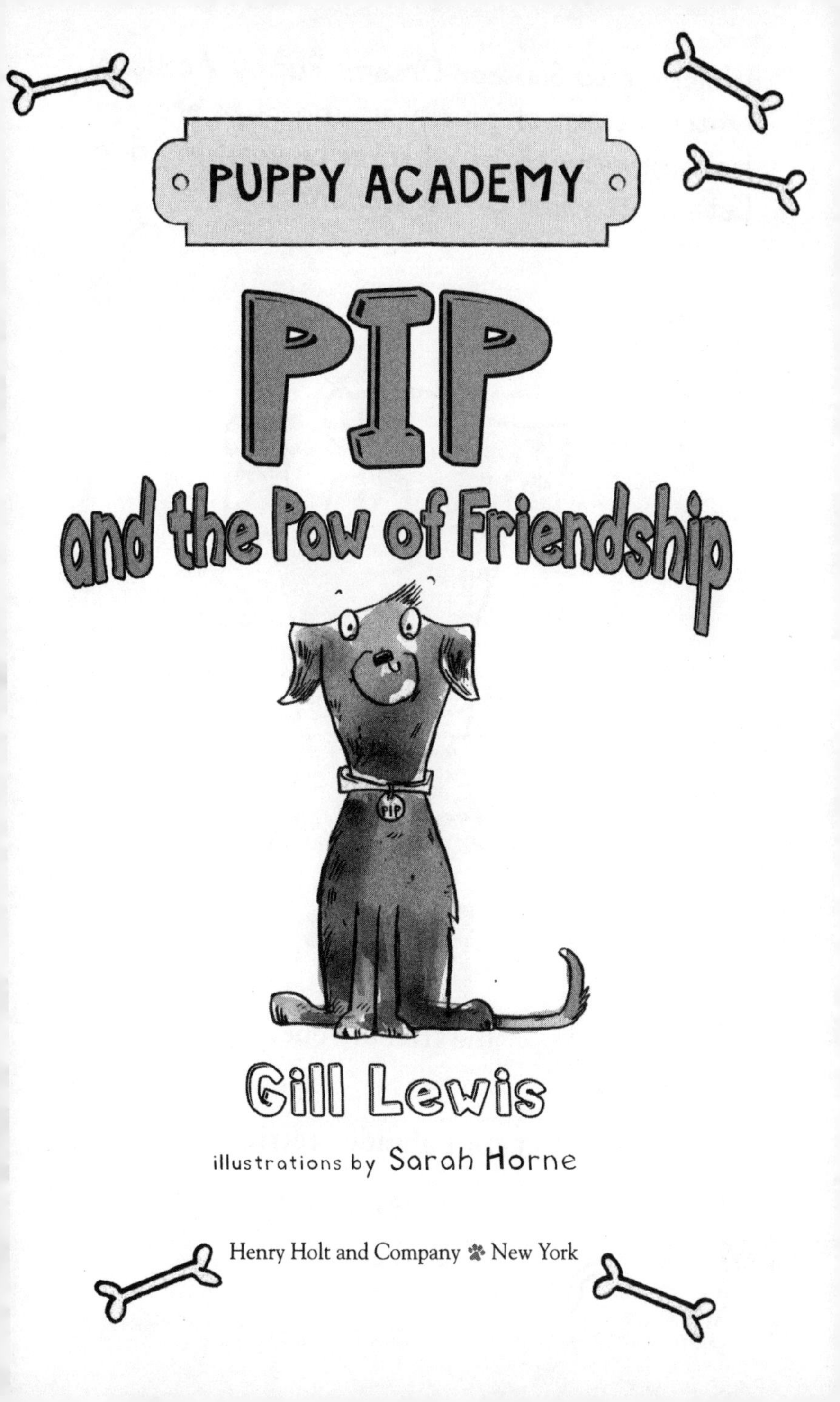

PUPPY ACADEMY

PIP and the Paw of Friendship

Gill Lewis

illustrations by Sarah Horne

Henry Holt and Company ❖ New York

Welcome to Sausage Dreams Puppy Academy, where a team of plucky young pups are learning how to be all sorts of working dogs. Let's meet some of the students . . .

the friendly one!

BREED: Labrador retriever

SPECIAL SKILL:

Ball games

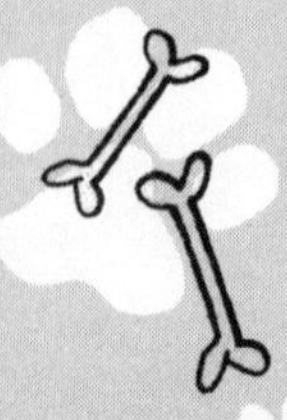

the smart one!

BREED: German shepherd

SPECIAL SKILL:
Sniffing out
crime

PA

the speedy one!

BREED: Border collie

SPECIAL SKILL:
Sensing danger

PA

MURPHY

the big one!

BREED: Leonberger

SPECIAL SKILL:
Swimming

PA

... and some of the teachers:

PA
PROFESSOR
OFFENBACH
Head of the Sausage
Dreams Puppy Academy.
She is a small dog with
A VERY LOUD VOICE!

1

The smell of sausages wafted along the line of puppies sitting in a neat row and drifted into Pip's nostrils. A sausage smothered in thick gravy lay in front of each pup. Saliva dripped from Pip's mouth and formed a large pool at his feet.

Pip willed himself not to look. He tried not to sniff the rising steam swirling deliciously around his nose. He tried to ignore the sausage that was asking to be eaten.

He glanced at the large bloodhound holding up his stopwatch.

"One minute to go," barked Major Bones.

One whole minute! thought Pip. It felt like a lifetime.

Pip looked along the line of puppies. No one had given in to the

sausages . . . yet. Maybe they would all earn their Resist Temptation badges. He hoped they would. They had been practicing hard.

They were pupils at the Sausage Dreams Puppy Academy for Working Dogs, where puppies trained for all sorts of important jobs. Some pups wanted to be police dogs. Others wanted to be sheepdogs. There were so many different jobs to choose from.

But Pip knew what he wanted to be. He was a Labrador retriever and wanted to be an assistance dog for a human, just like his mom and dad. His mom was a guide dog for the blind, and his dad was an assistance dog for the deaf. Pip wanted to help people too. He knew that the training was hard and that many dogs didn't make it through.

Every day, he dreamed of receiving the Paw of Friendship, a badge to show that he was an assistance dog and could help a human of his very own.

But first there were many tests to pass and badges to earn, beginning with the Resist Temptation badge. Pip had to pass if he wanted to be an assistance dog. His mom and dad were

watching with the other parents in the academy hall.

Major Bones, one of the teachers, was counting down the time. “Twenty seconds to go . . . nineteen . . . eighteen . . .”

Next to Pip, a little pug puppy licked his lips. His nose twitched. His eyes kept sliding down to look at the sausage.

"Hold on, Roly," whispered Pip. "Be strong."

Roly's tongue lolled out and dangled above the sausage.

"Don't do it, Roly. Hold your nerve. Not long now," said Pip.

Roly's eyes fixed on the sausage. "It's calling my name," he whimpered.

"Resist the sausage, Roly! Don't look at it. You can do it."

Major Bones blew the whistle.

PHHHHREEEEEW! "Time's up. Well done, pups. That was a very difficult test, indeed. We'll have a break before we do the final temptation test."

Roly dived on his sausage and slurped it up in a single gulp. "Thank you, Pip," he said, wiping gravy from his chin. "I don't know what I would have done without your help."

"That's okay," said Pip. "I wonder what the next test will be."

Pip was worried. Would it be Ginger the old tomcat, or Peter the mail carrier? Some dogs just couldn't help themselves when it came to chasing mail carriers. But Pip didn't mind cats or mail carriers. He never felt like chasing them at all.

There was one temptation, however, that Pip hoped he wouldn't face in the next test. There was one thing he couldn't resist. He just had to hope it would be something else.

"When you're ready, pups," barked Major Bones.

The pups lined up again as Major Bones brought a small box into the hall. "Inside here, I have something that many of you dream of chasing."

Too small for a mail carrier, thought Pip. Maybe Ginger was inside the box.

Major Bones reached inside.

Pip closed his eyes. He didn't want to see what it was. If he didn't know, he couldn't chase it.

BOING . . . BOING . . . BOING!

Pip's eyes snapped open. It was the unmistakable sound of a . . .

TENNIS BALL.

Pip was in the air, leaping for the ball. He snatched it and spun in midair, his legs running as he hit the ground. He raced around the hall with the ball in his teeth, daring anyone to chase him for it.

"PIP!" Major Bones was charging after him.

Pip ran faster, round and round and round. He had the ball, and he wasn't going to let anyone else get it.

"PIP! Stop at once!"

Pip stopped. He dropped the ball and looked around. He suddenly remembered where he was and what he was supposed to be doing. But it was too late. His mom and dad had their heads in their paws. Everyone else was just staring at him. What had he done?

Major Bones shook his head sadly.

"I'm sorry," said Pip. "Let me take the test again. Give me a cat or a squirrel instead."

"You can't take the test again. I'm sorry, Pip," said Major Bones. "You have to resist *all* temptations. What if you had led a blind person into a busy road just because you wanted to play ball on the other side?"

Pip hung his head. Major Bones was right. It didn't matter if he could resist sausages and cats and mail carriers. If he couldn't stop himself from joining in a ball game, he'd be no use to anyone.

He couldn't bring himself to look

at his mom and dad again. He turned from them and ran.

He'd messed up in one of the very first tests.

His dreams of being an assistance dog were over before his real training had even begun.

2

"I'm sorry," said Suli. "Maybe you could be a sniffer dog, or a search and rescue dog."

"I only want to be an assistance dog," wailed Pip. "What's wrong with me, Suli? Why can't I stop myself from chasing balls?"

"Well, it's good news for us," woofed Star. "We need you in the pawball final next week. Come on, Pip, we've got to run. Gruff Barking and the other teammates are waiting for us on the field."

Pip followed Suli and Star. He didn't feel like joining in, but all that changed the moment he saw the ball in the middle of the pawball field.

It was waiting just for him.

PPPHHHREWWWWW! Gruff Barking, the Puppy Academy sports teacher, blew his whistle for the training to begin.

Pip was off even before the whistle finished sounding. He dribbled the ball between his paws, in and out of the cones. Ahead he could see Star racing into the goal. Star was a border collie pup with lightning feet—and one of the best goalies in the academy. Pip knew he had to get in close before he tried to score.

Left paw . . . right paw . . . left paw . . . right paw . . . Pip took the ball forward, looking for an opening. Nosey, a Jack Russell terrier, dived for the ball, and Lulu, a poodle, tried to tackle, but Pip skipped past them both and knocked the ball into the air. Star jumped for it, but Pip's nose reached the ball first, sending it flying into the goal.

PPPHHHREWWWW! "Well done, pups, well done." Gruff Barking called all the pups together. "Great practice session. You'll need to play like that next week when we're up against the MadDogz in the pawball final."

The five pups of the pawball team looked at one another. The puppies of the MadDogz team were the unbeaten champions. They were young guard dogs from the Security Dog School on the other side of town. They all looked big and scary. It was rumored that Exterminator, their goalie, wasn't even allowed out without a muzzle.

"Do we *have* to play them?" asked Suli. Suli was a saluki pup. What she lacked in strength, she made up for in speed and in her midair turns.

Gruff Barking looked slowly around at them. "MadDogz have been beaten before," he said.

"That was ten years ago," said Lulu. "They've held the Golden Ball in their trophy cabinet ever since."

"They can be beaten again," said Gruff Barking. "You've gotten to the final, so you have a chance of winning. Come on, pups, you can do this. Don't forget who you are!"

"Give me an *S*," woofed Star.

"Give me a *D*," barked Suli.

"Give me a *P*," yapped Lulu.

"Give me an *A*," yipped Nosey.

"Who are we?" The pups high-fived one another and barked, "We're the Sausage Dreams Puppy Academy!"

Pip joined in, but he couldn't help thinking that they didn't sound very tough compared to the MadDogz.

PPPHHHREWWWW! Gruff Barking blew his whistle again. "Right, pups," he said. "Let's try some nose balances."

Pip was just perfecting balancing the ball on the tip of his nose when

Major Bones arrived on the playing field with Pip's mom and dad.

Pip dropped the ball and stared down at his feet. "I'm sorry I didn't pass the test," he said.

"It doesn't matter," said Pip's mom.

"But it does matter," wailed Pip. "I can't take the test again."

Pip's dad sat down next to him. "How much do you want to be an assistance dog?"

"More than anything," said Pip.

Pip's mom and dad looked at each other, and then at Major Bones. "Well, if that's really what you want," said Pip's mom, "Major Bones says he will let you take the test again."

"Really?" asked Pip.

"Really," said Pip's mom.

"That's right," said Major Bones. "But before you take the test, we must be sure you are ready. We have to stop you from chasing balls or playing any ball games."

Pip stared at Major Bones. "Even pawball?"

"Yes." Major Bones nodded. "It's the only way."

"No!" gasped Pip.

"He can't leave us," woofed Star.

"We're playing against the MadDogz next week," wailed Lulu. "We need Pip!"

Major Bones shook his head. "If Pip really wants to be an assistance dog, he'll have to give up pawball."

"For good?" whispered Pip.

Gruff Barking's whiskers bristled. "Can't it wait until next week? We need Pip in the final."

"I'm afraid not," said Major Bones. "I've just heard that a place has opened up at the training center for assistance dogs. Pip has been invited there for a trial period on Monday."

Pip looked around at his teammates. "I'm sorry," he said.

"You don't have to go," said Star.

"But I do," said Pip.

"You don't have to be an assistance dog," said Lulu. "You're so good at pawball; you could turn professional. You could be famous and travel the world."

Pip shook his head. "I love pawball, but I don't want to play it forever. I love people more. One day, I want to make a difference in someone's life. One day, I want to wear the Paw of Friendship on my collar," he said. "I'll do whatever it takes, even if it means putting my pawball days behind me."

"WELCOME TO ANOTHER FRIDAY AWARD CEREMONY," woofed Professor Offenbach. **"PLEASE SIT!"** Professor Offenbach was the head of the Sausage Dreams Puppy Academy for Working Dogs. She was a small dog with a big voice. Even Major Bones sometimes had to tie his ears beneath his chin when she was talking. **"IT'S BEEN ANOTHER SUCCESSFUL WEEK AT THE ACADEMY, AND I HAVE SEVERAL AWARDS AND WORK PLACEMENTS TO GIVE OUT TODAY."**

Pip sat with his friends and watched other pups climb onto the giant sausage podium to collect their awards and badges.

"CONGRATULATIONS TO DUCHESS FOR HER CATTLE HERDING LEVEL-ONE BADGE," woofed Professor Offenbach, hanging a badge around Duchess's neck. "DUCHESS IS VERY LUCKY AS WE'VE JUST HEARD THAT SHE WILL BE VISITING THE ROYAL COWS FOR HER LEVEL-TWO BADGE."

The corgi pup puffed out her chest in pride and readjusted her tiara. She was from a long line of royal corgis.

"AND FINALLY," boomed Professor Offenbach, **"I WOULD LIKE TO PRESENT THE FOLLOWING PUPS WITH THE RESIST TEMPTATION BADGE. . . ."**

Roly leaned across to Pip. "I'm sorry you didn't pass the test."

"That's okay, Roly," said Pip. "Don't worry about me."

"It's me I'm worried about," whispered Roly. "Gruff Barking's making me play in the pawball final in your place."

"You'll be fine," said Pip.

"Fine?" said Roly. "Have you seen the size of the MadDogz team?

They'll eat us alive . . . literally."

Star gave Pip a nudge. Professor Offenbach was glaring right at him.

"IT SEEMS THAT PIP CAN'T RESIST THE TEMPTATION TO TALK AS WELL AS PLAY BALL GAMES."

Pip tucked his tail between his legs.

He watched his friends climb onto the podium and receive their badges. He wished he could join them up there too. Maybe he would one day. He hoped so. But he knew he wouldn't be joining them on the sports field next week. He sighed and tried not to think about the final. It felt as if part of him had gone. His pawball days were well and truly over.

3

Pip climbed into the minibus next to Major Bones, ready for the journey to the Helping Paws Training Center in the city.

His friends had come to wave good-bye.

"See you soon," woofed Star.

The minibus rumbled to life and trundled down the hill, away from Sausage Dreams Puppy Academy.

Pip pushed his nose out of the

window. "Good luck in the final!" he barked.

"Bye, Pip!"

"Bye!"

Pip waved and waved as the academy disappeared into the distance. The hills and fields were replaced by shops and houses as they drove into the city. The smells of car fumes and burger joints drifted in through the open window. It was noisy too. There were so many humans in the city. There were no fields to play

in. At least there wouldn't be any ball games to tempt him.

"We're here," announced Major Bones, pulling into the parking lot of the Helping Paws Training Center.

"Welcome," woofed a large yellow Labrador. "Welcome."

"Colonel Custard!" said Major Bones, shaking the yellow Labrador's paw.

Colonel Custard was the head of the training center. He was a retired assistance dog with a graying muzzle, a rickety hip, and a fondness for custard creams. What he didn't know about being an assistance dog wasn't worth knowing.

Major Bones rummaged in the back of the minibus. "Professor Offenbach sent you these," he said, holding out a packet of custard creams. "She knows how much you love them."

"Not for me," said Colonel Custard, patting his tummy. "I must resist. The vets have put me on a custard cream restriction diet. They're not good for the old hip." Colonel Custard looked down at sn't worth knowing.

Major Bones rummaged in the :k of the minibus. "Professor 'enbach sent you these," he said, ding out a packet of custard ıms. "She knows how much you : them."

Not for me," said Colonel :ard, patting his tummy. "I must resist. The vets have put me on a custard cream restriction diet. They're not good for the old hip." Colonel Custard looked down at

3

Pip climbed into the minibus next to Major Bones, ready for the journey to the Helping Paws Training Center in the city.

His friends had come to wave good-bye.

"See you soon," woofed Star.

The minibus rumbled to life and trundled down the hill, away from Sausage Dreams Puppy Academy.

Pip pushed his nose out of the

window. "Good luck in the final!" he barked.

"Bye, Pip!"

"Bye!"

Pip waved and waved as the academy disappeared into the distance. The hills and fields were replaced by shops and houses as they drove into the city. The smells of car fumes and burger joints drifted in through the open window. It was noisy too. There were so many humans in the city. There were no fields to play

in. At least there would
ball games to tempt hir

"We're here," annou
Bones, pulling into the
the Helping Paws Trai

"Welcome," woofed
Labrador. "Welcome.

"Colonel Custard!
Bones, shaking the y
paw.

Colonel Custard
of the training cent
retired assistance d
muzzle, a rickety h
for custard creams
know about being

Pip. "So this is our new recruit, eh?" He gave Pip a good, long look. "So, you're the pawball player?"

"*Ex*-pawball player," said Pip sadly.

Major Bones turned to Pip. "Colonel Custard was once the rising star of the Junior Pawball League," he said.

Pip's eyes opened wide. "Really?"

"It's true," said Colonel Custard, a faraway look in his eye. "I could nose a ball into the goal from ten yards away, doing a half spin." He sighed. "I had to give it all up, though."

"What happened?" asked Pip.

Colonel Custard tapped his leg.

"Bad hips, I'm afraid. That's when I became an assistance dog instead."

"Didn't you miss pawball?" said Pip.

"Not after I met Andy." Colonel Custard smiled as they walked inside. He took out a photo of a man in a wheelchair. "Andy said I saved him, but it was Andy who saved me. Being an assistance dog to him was the best thing in the world."

Pip's training began with the washing machine. He put his head inside and grabbed a wet towel, pulling it out onto the floor.

"Let's try to get it in the laundry basket this time," said Colonel Custard.

Pip tried again.

All morning, Pip learned new skills. He learned how to open drawers and cupboards. He learned how to take socks off someone's feet and undo zippers on coats. There was so much to know.

"Try the pedestrian crossing button,"

said Colonel Custard. “You might not be tall enough yet.”

Pip did a high leap and a turn and slapped the button with his paw.

“Well done,” cheered Colonel Custard. “You’re a very fast learner. I think you will make an excellent assistance dog.”

Pip puffed out his chest in pride.

Colonel Custard rubbed his chin. “In fact,” he said, “I know a human who might be your perfect match.”

“Really?” said Pip. He could hardly believe it.

"Yes," said Colonel Custard. "You would still have to complete your training at the academy, but I may be able to introduce you to your human tomorrow." He held up a photograph. "This is Kayla. She needs an assistance dog."

Pip stared at the photo of a young girl in a wheelchair. "A human of my very own?"

Colonel Custard hurriedly put the photo away. "It all depends, of course," he said, his voice sounding very serious, "if you can forget all about pawball and ball games. Do you think you can do that?"

"I'll try," said Pip. "I'll try my very best."

"Did you sleep well?" asked Colonel Custard over a bowl of Crunchie Munchies the next morning.

"Yes," lied Pip. He hadn't slept well. He'd had dreams of tennis balls and custard creams and Kayla, all whirling in his head.

"Good," said Colonel Custard, "because today we're going to help you to resist tennis balls, footballs, and soccer balls. You name it, we'll get you to resist it."

"But how?"

"As you know," said Colonel Custard, "I have a fondness for custard creams. I can hardly resist them. So when I want a custard cream, I try to imagine something really big and scary between myself and the custard cream."

"Like what?" said Pip.

"Well . . . like a crocodile."

"A crocodile?"

"It doesn't have to be a crocodile . . . just think of something scary."

Pip thought hard. He thought of Exterminator on the MadDogz team. He thought of Exterminator's huge fangs and wild eyes.

"Here we go," said Colonel Custard. He rolled a ball across the ground. Pip imagined Exterminator standing in front of him. But all Pip wanted to do was get the ball himself. He launched at the ball and dribbled it away.

"No, no, no!" said Colonel Custard.

"You need to think of something *really* terrifying."

Pip closed his eyes and thought hard. He tried to imagine the most frightening thing. And then he realized what it was. The thing that scared him most was the thought of never meeting Kayla.

"I'm ready," said Pip.

Colonel Custard rolled ball after ball across the ground, but Pip didn't chase one of them. He pictured Kayla in his mind and knew that if he chased just one of the balls, he would never get the chance to be her assistance dog.

"Well done." Colonel Custard beamed. "I think you are ready to meet Kayla."

At the end of the afternoon, Pip sat in Colonel Custard's office, munching on a custard cream.

"Kayla will arrive any minute now," said Colonel Custard. "I think you'll be perfect together. I've paired assistance dogs to their humans for many years, and I've never gotten a match wrong yet."

Pip's paws tingled with excitement. He wondered what Kayla would be like.

There was a knock on the office door.

"Come in," woofed Colonel Custard.

The door pushed open very slowly, and in came a young girl using a wheelchair, followed by a tall woman.

"Pip, this is Kayla and her mother," said Colonel Custard.

Pip bounded over to meet Kayla. She was going to be his human! The girl threw her arms up in the air. Surely this meant she wanted to meet him. She wanted him to jump up and lick her face.

Up Pip bounced, again and again, springing higher and higher.

Kayla flapped her hands in the air.

"HELLO, HELLO, HELLO!" Pip barked.

But Kayla couldn't understand his woofs and barks. All she heard was, "WOOF, WOOF, WOOF!"

"Take him away!" she screamed. "Take that dog away!"

Pip ran from the room, his tail between his legs. Kayla didn't like him. Somehow he'd messed things up. But how?

In spite of all Colonel Custard's years of matching dogs and humans, maybe he'd gotten this match horribly, horribly wrong.

4

"Not to worry," said Colonel Custard, patting Pip on the back.

"She hates me," wailed Pip.

"She doesn't understand you," said Colonel Custard. "She's never met a puppy before."

"But I said hello," said Pip.

Colonel Custard sighed. "Humans don't understand everything we say with our woofs and barks. She thought you were attacking her, bouncing around like that. Humans have to learn what we say with our bodies. If we wag our tails, we're happy. If our tails are tucked between our legs, we're sad or frightened. Sometimes we have to tell them things with our eyes."

"With our eyes?" said Pip. "What do you mean?"

Colonel Custard smiled. "There are no lessons for that, young Pip. You'll just find out how yourself one day."

Pip looked at all the people in the street. Humans were confusing. Maybe the lessons on how to get to

know them would be the hardest lessons of all.

"Let's try again," said Colonel Custard. "We'll be meeting Kayla in her house this time. When you greet Kayla, sit down, wag your tail, and wait for her to come to you."

"Okay," said Pip. He followed Colonel Custard along the streets to Kayla's house, feeling smart in his fluorescent yellow training jacket and training collar.

"Remember, don't jump up or bounce around," said Colonel Custard.

Pip nodded, although he thought it would be hard to stay still for so long. "Can't Kayla walk at all?" he said.

Colonel Custard shook his head. "Kayla was injured in an accident. That's why she uses a wheelchair now," he said. "She's had many operations on her back, and she hasn't been able to go to school for a long time."

No school? thought Pip. He'd hate it if he couldn't go to the Puppy Academy. He'd feel so lonely. "Doesn't she miss her friends?" said Pip.

Colonel Custard sighed. "It's been very hard for her to go through all those operations, and all that time in the hospital has made it difficult to keep in touch with friends. Her mother said she's lost contact with most of them, and that's been the hardest thing of all."

"We're here," announced Colonel Custard.

Kayla lived with her mother in a small white bungalow. Out front there was a garden filled with pots of brightly colored flowers. A path beside the bungalow led to shops and the park beyond. Pip waited nervously for Kayla's mother to open the door. Would they let him inside after yesterday?

"Come in," said Kayla's mother with a smile, leading them to the kitchen. She sat down next to Pip and stroked his head. "Look, Kayla," she said. "Pip's a friendly puppy."

Pip wagged his tail even faster.

Kayla glared suspiciously at Pip. "I'm fine," she snapped. "I don't need a stupid dog to help me." She turned her wheelchair around and left the room.

Pip didn't know what to do. He stared after Kayla. How could he be an assistance dog if his human didn't want his help?

Kayla's mother looked at Pip and nodded after Kayla. "Go on, Pip," she said. "Go and find her."

Pip trotted through the doorway, following Kayla to her bedroom at the end of the hall. Kayla slammed the door behind her, shutting Pip out.

Pip knew all about doors now. He stood up on his

hind legs, pulled the handle, and let himself in.

Kayla was sitting at her desk. "Go away, puppy."

Pip sat down beside her.

Kayla glared at him. "Have it your way," she said, "but I don't need your help."

Pip watched Kayla take her pens and pencils out from the drawers on her desk. She had everything at hand. Maybe she didn't need him. She'd managed so far without his help.

Pip lay down next to her and closed his eyes. It was warm with the sun streaming through the window. It was so warm that he began to drift into sleep.

Pip woke up to find pencils and paper raining down on him, and Kayla reaching to grab them back.

The pencils scattered across the floor and under the bed.

Pip picked up a pencil in his mouth and offered it to Kayla, but she crumpled up her picture and threw it in the trash can.

"It was a bad drawing anyway." She frowned.

Pip pushed the pencil onto Kayla's lap.

"I don't want it," said Kayla. She turned away and stared out the window.

Pip collected all the pencils one by one. He had to reach beneath the bed for the last few. He pushed one into Kayla's hand.

Kayla's fingers wrapped around the pencil, and she turned to Pip. "You don't give up, do you?"

Pip wagged his tail.

"So, you think I should draw another picture?"

"Yes," woofed Pip. "Yes."

Kayla sat and looked at Pip for a long time before she began another drawing.

When Kayla struggled to reach a pencil sharpener from a low drawer, Pip opened the drawer for her. When Pip felt Kayla's hands were cold, he fetched her fleecy jacket from her closet.

All the time, Kayla worked on her drawing. When she finished, she held it up for Pip to see.

"What do you think?" she said.

"It's me," woofed Pip.

Kayla leaned forward and reached out her hand.

Pip pushed his head into her hand and let her gently stroke his soft ears. "Good pup," she whispered.

Pip wagged his tail faster and faster. Kayla liked him. She was beginning to trust him, and it was the best feeling in the world.

For the rest of the day, Pip wouldn't leave Kayla's side. He fetched things she couldn't reach. He helped pull her socks off and find her slippers. He even helped her taste some cookies she made. In the afternoon, he and Kayla played in the garden, and in the evening they cuddled up on the sofa and watched a movie together. At bedtime, Pip pulled the covers over Kayla to keep her warm and fetched her book. He jumped up on the bed and leaned against her while she read him a story about a girl named Opal and a dog named Winn-Dixie.

"Good night, Kayla, good night, Pip," said Kayla's mother. She kissed them both and switched off the

light. Pip curled up beside Kayla on the bed. She was his very own human, and he'd do anything for her.

"Pip?" whispered Kayla.

Pip put his head in Kayla's hand.

"I'm sorry I didn't like you at first," she said. "I was just scared, that's all."

Pip whined and licked her hand.

Kayla sighed. "It's as if you understand everything I say."

"I do," said Pip. "You don't know that, but I do."

"You're my best friend, Pip," said Kayla. She hugged him tight and buried her head in his neck. Pip could feel her hot tears slide into his fur. “My only friend.”

5

"Excellent!" Colonel Custard smiled. "Excellent. Just as I'd hoped. A perfect match."

Colonel Custard sat with Pip in Kayla's kitchen the next day and ticked off the task boxes on his list. "Open doors . . . tick . . . remove socks from feet . . . tick . . . pick up dropped items . . . tick . . ." He looked up at Pip. "This is very good, indeed," he woofed, ticking off box after box.

Pip wagged his tail. He was pleased he was doing so well. He knew that he would need more training and wouldn't be able to stay with Kayla yet, but they would meet up again several times until he was old enough to be her full-time assistance dog.

"Just one more test," said Colonel Custard, "to make sure you are the right dog for Kayla."

"What test is that?" asked Pip.

Colonel Custard frowned. "It's the most important test of all. It isn't easy, but I think you are ready for it. You must take Kayla up the street, across the main road, past the shops, along the bottom of the park, and back home. You will be crossing busy roads, and you must help Kayla to stay safe. Do well, and you will be Kayla's assistance dog for life. Fail this test, and I'm afraid we'll have to find another assistance dog for Kayla."

"I can do this," Pip woofed.

Colonel Custard smiled. "I'm sure you can."

"I'm not going anywhere," shouted Kayla. "You can't make me."

"It's only around the block. You'll be fine. . . ." began Kayla's mother.

"I'm staying right here," yelled Kayla.

Her mother tried to hand her Pip's leash. "Kayla . . ."

"I'm not going anywhere. Ever." Kayla spun her wheelchair around and stormed to her bedroom, slamming the door behind her.

Kayla's mother sighed and sat down. She put her head in her hands. "I don't know what to do,

Pip. I just don't know what to do."

Pip picked up the leash in his mouth. He had an idea but wasn't sure it would work. He trotted along the hallway and let himself into Kayla's room. He found her sobbing by the window.

Kayla stroked his soft ears and buried her head in his fur. "No one understands, Pip," she cried. "I've hardly been out of the house in the last few years, except to the hospital. I haven't been anywhere on my own before. Not even to the park. What will I say if I meet anyone? What will I do? I'm too scared to face the world right now."

Pip dropped the end of the leash onto Kayla's lap and looked up at her. "Don't be scared, Kayla," he said with his deep brown eyes. "You're not alone because I'm with you now. Trust me. We'll go out and face the world together."

Kayla wrapped her fingers around the leash and looked into Pip's eyes for a long, long time. Then she wiped her eyes and smiled.

"Come on, then, Pip," she said, giving his head a rub. "You and I are going out, together."

"Woof!" said Pip. "Woof!" Maybe

this was what Colonel Custard meant by talking with your eyes. Sometimes it seemed as if his human could understand everything he said.

“Be back before dark,” said Colonel Custard, tapping his watch. “Major Bones will be here to see you finish your test.”

Pip and Kayla set off together down the street. Pip could sense her excitement and worry through her tight hold on his leash.

It was busy. People moved aside to let them pass on the sidewalk. All

Pip could see were people's legs and tummies. It was hard to see their faces. He thought Kayla's view from the wheelchair must be the same for her too.

Pip stopped at the crosswalk. The traffic was busy, whizzing past. Kayla let Pip leap up and pat his paw on the button, then they both waited until the green man showed that they could cross.

"Good, Pip," said Kayla.

Pip looked up at Kayla to see she was smiling. They were both enjoying this walk today.

"Let's go to the corner store, Pip,

shall we?" said Kayla. "I'll buy some cookies."

"I like cookies," woofed Pip, although he knew he wasn't allowed too many of them.

Pip walked next to Kayla up the side ramp to the store. The door was stiff to open, so Pip put his paws up and helped to push it wide enough for Kayla's wheelchair to get through. Inside the store, Kayla chose the packet of cookies she wanted. She counted out the money and let Pip put his paws up on the counter to pass her purse to the shopkeeper. The shopkeeper offered Pip a dog treat, but Pip didn't take it. He was a working dog now. He walked with Kayla down the ramp toward the park, his head held high.

They were almost home. Pip could see Kayla's house in the distance. There were no more roads to cross now. All they had to do was walk along the park to reach the path to the bungalow. Pip wagged his tail. He and Kayla were a great team.

The park was busy. There were people walking their dogs and others flying kites. On the far side, Pip could see a group of children playing a game on a rectangle of concrete. A ball bounced on the ground.

BOING . . . BOING . . . BOING!

Pip's paws twitched. His tail tingled with excitement. The children were running around, bouncing the ball and throwing it between them. It looked a bit like pawball, except the children had to get the ball into netted hoops on the top of very high poles. Two of the children chased the ball as it left the court and rolled across the grass.

Pip stopped to watch, pulling at his leash.

"Basketball," said Kayla. "Looks fun, doesn't it?"

"Looks fun?" said Pip. "It looks BRILLIANT!"

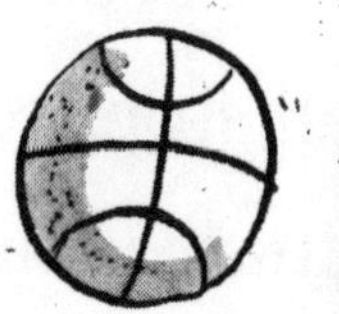

BOING . . . BOING, BOING . . .

Pip bounded forward, pulling the leash from Kayla's hand. "Come on, Kayla," he woofed. "Let's play!" He was off, racing across the park toward the ball. He scooped up the ball on his nose, spinning it in the air, and then he ran to the children, dribbling the

ball between his paws. The children all stopped and pointed, then they charged after him. One boy flung himself on the ground, hitting the ball away from Pip. It flew upward and across the top of the hoop, missing it by inches.

The children threw the ball for Pip again. Pip stopped it with his paw and looked back toward Kayla. She was sitting where he'd left her. "Woof!" he barked. Why didn't she want to join in too? "Woof!"

But Kayla turned her wheelchair around and started heading toward home.

"Woof!" barked Pip. He didn't

want to let go of the ball now that he had it, so he ran across the park toward Kayla, dribbling it between his paws. Behind him, he could hear the children chasing after him. Pip stopped in front of Kayla.

"You left me, Pip," she said. "You left me to be with them."

Pip could see tears in her eyes.

"No," said Pip. He looked at her with his deep brown eyes. "I came back because I want you to play too."

"Is this your dog?"

Pip looked up. He and Kayla were surrounded by a sea of faces.

"He's so cute!"

"Is he yours?"

"He's cool."

"Can I pet him?"

"What's his name?"

"Did you teach him to play basketball?"

"Can he do other tricks?"

"How long have you had him?"

"Do you live around here?"

"I'm Haya."

"I'm Ali."

"I'm Jake."

"I'm Cintra."

"I'm Sophie."

"I'm Luke."

"What's your name?"

"I'm Kayla," said Kayla, stroking Pip's ears. "And this is Pip."

"Cool!" said Haya. "Do you want to play?"

Pip pushed the ball into Kayla's hands. "Woof!" he said, answering for both of them.

Kayla and the children followed Pip across the grass to the basketball court.

"Kayla! Be on our team," yelled Sophie.

The children spread out across the court. Kayla held the ball in her hands. She didn't know what to do.

"Woof!" barked Pip. "Over here."

Kayla flung the ball, and Pip was off, dribbling it forward. Cintra managed to get the ball from Pip and ran with it, bouncing it up the court, but she was intercepted by Luke, who flung it down the far side to Jake.

Kayla spun her wheelchair round and round, following the ball, hitting it in midair when it passed her, or catching it and passing it on.

"Hey, Pip," yelled Kayla. "Catch!"

Pip jumped and spun the ball on his nose before passing it.

"You're good, Kayla!" woofed Pip. "A natural!"

The children played basketball late into the afternoon, only stopping when Kayla shared her cookies with everyone. The sun was setting, and dark shadows slunk across the field.

"Last game," Ali shouted.

He ran with the ball, dodging between the others, bouncing it close beside him. Pip leaped in and tapped the ball away.

"Hey!" called Jake.

But Pip was already bouncing down toward the other hoop.

Kayla charged after him, dirt flying up behind her wheels, faster and faster. "I'm with you, Pip," she yelled.

Pip was almost there, the other team hot on his heels. Pip and Kayla raced together side by side.

"Woof!" Pip barked, sending the ball up into the air.

Kayla spun around.

Pip saw Kayla reaching for the ball, her wheels spinning beneath her.

Spinning, spinning, spinning.

She was going fast—too fast. Her hand punched the ball, and it flew in an arc in the air. Kayla lost control as her wheelchair flipped and toppled over. Kayla hit the ground as the ball fell right in through the hoop, winning them the game.

"PIP!"

Pip turned. In the gathering gloom, he could see Colonel Custard, Major Bones, and Kayla's mother all running toward them.

Pip looked back at Kayla lying on the ground. He could see grazes on her elbows. He hadn't gotten her home before dark. He hadn't kept her safe. She was hurt, and it was all his fault.

He had failed.

He couldn't resist a ball game.

He would never be an assistance dog now.

Worse still, he would never see Kayla ever again.

6

Back at the academy, Pip's teammates tried to cheer him up.

"At least you're back in time for the final tomorrow," said Star.

"Let's talk about our tactics," said Nosey.

"Come on, Pip," said Lulu. "We'll need to have a plan if we want to beat the MadDogz. They won their semifinal round, fifty goals to zero."

"And the other team's goalie

ended up at the vets'," said Suli.

Pip joined the others, but his heart wasn't in it. All he could think about was Kayla and how he'd let her down. Pawball just didn't seem important anymore.

"WELCOME, WELCOME, EVERYONE!" Professor Offenbach's voice boomed out over the playing field. **"WE ARE VERY LUCKY TODAY TO BE HOSTING THE PAWBALL FINAL HERE AT SAUSAGE DREAMS PUPPY ACADEMY."**

Cheers erupted from the crowd. Dogs from the neighborhood and the academy had turned out to watch the match.

"LET'S GIVE A BIG CHEER FOR OUR OWN SAUSAGE DREAMS PUPPY ACADEMY TEAM!"

All the puppies went wild, howling and barking as Pip and his team ran onto the field.

"AND LET US SAY A VERY BIG WELCOME TO THE REIGNING CHAMPIONS . . . THE MADDOGZ!"

A hush fell across the crowd as the MadDogz ran on. Pip had never seen them up close before.

The puppies of the MadDogz team were huge, great beasts, with sharp teeth and wild eyes. They looked like full-grown dogs. Exterminator, their goalie, bounded on last. Some of the pups booed, and Exterminator bared his teeth at them. *He isn't a dog*, thought Pip. *He's a monster*. He was so big that he filled up the whole goal area. There'd be no way to get a ball past him.

For the first half of the match, Pip and his teammates spent most of the time running away from the ball. The MadDogz were heavy and slow, but they were scary. Pip didn't dare challenge any of them.

When the halftime whistle blew, the MadDogz were up, twenty to nothing. Pip joined his teammates for a bowl of water. "I wish it could be over," he said.

"I'd rather die than go back out there," wailed Lulu.

"They're not dogs; they're wild animals," said Nosey.

The puppies huddled together

and watched the MadDogz team strutting on the field.

"Who's that?" said Star.

The pups looked across the playing field to see an old yellow Labrador hobbling toward them, followed by a girl using a wheelchair and a group of children.

"It's Colonel Custard and the children from the park," barked Pip, jumping up. "And Kayla. It's Kayla!"

"Hello, young pups," said Colonel Custard.

"I couldn't resist coming to a pawball match. Kayla and her friends wanted to come with me too." He sighed happily. "It reminds me of my Junior Pawball League days."

Pip pushed his face into Kayla's hands, and she stroked him while he sniffed at her wheelchair.

"It's new, I know," Kayla said, smiling. "My last one was damaged in that fall playing basketball. Anyway, I needed this one. See how its wheels are angled so they're much wider apart at the bottom? It won't tip over so easily. I'll need it because I've joined a wheelchair basketball team."

"That's great news," woofed Pip, wagging his tail.

"I know," smiled Kayla. "Haya's mom saw me shoot the ball into the hoop. She said I should take it up. There's a wheelchair basketball club near me. I'm going to play every week."

PPPHHHREWWWWW!

All the pups looked at one another. It was the start of the second half.

"I'm not going back in," said Suli.

"Me neither," said Nosey.

Pip tucked his tail between his legs and sat down.

"Pups!" said Colonel Custard. "This isn't fighting talk. The MadDogz are a bunch of softies."

"Softies! Have you seen the size of them?" said Star.

"They are big, it's true," said Colonel Custard. "But they are slow and heavy. Use your speed, use your turns, and you can win this game."

"What makes you so sure?" said Pip.

"Because," said Colonel Custard, holding up a photo, "I was on the team that won against the MadDogz ten years ago."

The pups stared at the faded photo of a lean yellow Labrador nosing the winning goal.

"Is that really you?" said Lulu.

Colonel Custard looked around at them all. "They could be beaten then, and you can beat them now."

Pip didn't feel so sure. He slunk around the other side of Kayla's wheelchair and put his head in Kayla's hands. "I'm scared, Kayla."

Kayla stroked his ears and looked deep into his eyes. "Don't be scared, Pip," she whispered. "When I was scared, you gave me courage. You stayed with me. Now I'm here for you. You're not alone, Pip, because I'm with you."

Pip felt his chest swell

up. He might not be Kayla's assistance dog, but he was still her friend, and that meant more than anything.

He would go out there and play his best. He'd do it for Kayla.

"Come on, team," he woofed. "Give me an *S*."

"Give me a *D*," barked Suli.

"Give me a *P*," yapped Lulu.

"Give me an *A*," yipped Nosey.

"Who are we?" barked Star.

The pups high-fived each other. "We're the Sausage Dreams Puppy Academy!"

7

The pups were fast. Star and Lulu whizzed the ball along the ground. Nosey was so small that she could run beneath the MadDogz puppies' legs. Suli's midair turns knocked ball after ball into the goal. The MadDogz were puffing and panting. Some had to stop to catch their breath. The score was twenty to twenty when the whistle blew for extra time.

It was the last chance to win the

match. Pip had the ball. He dribbled it along the sideline. But Exterminator was already in the goal, his hackles raised, saliva dripping from his fangs. How could Pip get past him? Exterminator rushed forward, and Pip nosed the ball high into the air.

Exterminator leaped, his paw outreached.

The ball skimmed the very tip

of one of Exterminator's claws and bounced against a goalpost, spinning into the goal.

The crowd howled and barked and cheered.

When the cheering had died down, Pip looked at Exterminator lying on the ground, clutching his paw and howling in pain.

Pip edged closer to him. “Are you all right?”

“Noooo,” howled Exterminator. He held up his paw. “I’ve split my claw and it huuurts!” he blubbered.

Jaws, the MadDogz team captain, had to sit down and look away. “I

don't like the sight of blood," he whined.

Colonel Custard arrived with the first aid kit for Exterminator's paw. "Just like I said," he woofed to Pip. "They're a bunch of big softies, really."

"INSTEAD OF THE FRIDAY AWARD CEREMONY, WE WILL PRESENT THE PAWBALL FINAL TROPHY. PLEASE COME TO THE GIANT SAUSAGE PODIUM, PIP, STAR, SULI, LULU, AND NOSEY," woofed Professor Offenbach.

Pip held up the Golden Ball with

his teammates. He could see Colonel Custard's name engraved in the trophy from ten years before.

All the puppies cheered.

"JUST ONE MORE THING," said Professor Offenbach, quieting them down. **"WE ARE VERY PROUD TO WELCOME COLONEL CUSTARD BACK TO THE ACADEMY. HE WOULD LIKE TO MAKE AN IMPORTANT ANNOUNCEMENT."**

Colonel Custard climbed onto the podium. "We have a very special pup among us," he said. "We have a champion pawball player. Now that Kayla is on the wheelchair basketball team, she will need help to prepare and train for matches. She has asked if Pip can be her assistance dog."

Pip felt his heart leap. He looked across at Kayla.

Star, Suli, Lulu, and Nosey cheered.

Colonel Custard cleared his throat. "But it's not just for his pawball skills that Kayla needs him. It's more than that. It's for the courage he gives her to make friends, have fun, and face the world."

Pip's paws trembled. Could it really be true that he would be an assistance dog for Kayla?

"And so," continued Colonel Custard, "I would like to present Pip with a very special award, given only to those dogs who dedicate their lives to helping humans. I'd like to present Pip with the Paw of Friendship."

Pip stood proudly while Colonel Custard clipped the Paw of Friendship to his collar, then he bounded over to Kayla.

She threw her arms around his neck and buried her head in his fur. "I've got lots of friends now, but you're my best friend of all. I love you, Pip," she said. "I always will."

"Woof," said Pip. He looked up at her and spoke with his big brown eyes. "And I love you too."

PUPPY PLEDGE

I promise to be honest, brave, and true and serve my fellow dogs and humans too.

In peril, I will be your guide, walking with you by your side.

I am your eyes, your ears, your nose, through wind and rain and sun and snow. I'll be with you until the very end, your wet-nosed, waggy-tailed best, best friend.

Meet Josie, a real-life assistance dog!

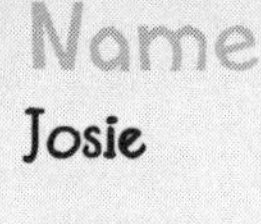

Name
Josie

Age
8

Occupation
Child's assistance dog

Likes
Ball games and tummy rubs

Hates
Brushing time!

Josie loves to fetch and pick up things for Sam, who has a severe disability. She's his forever friend. "I'd be lost without her," he says.

Assistance Dog Facts

There are many different types of assistance dogs, including hearing dogs, guide dogs for the blind, and dogs that help people with physical disabilities.

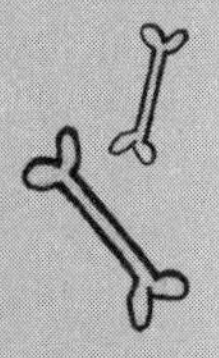

DID YOU KNOW?

It takes almost two years of training for a puppy to learn how to be an assistance dog.

Assistance dogs help give their owners confidence by enabling them to be more independent.

DID YOU KNOW?

Lots of assistance dogs are Labradors or golden retrievers.

When they retire, assistance dogs normally stay with their owner as a pet.

DID YOU KNOW?

In Italy, there is a 2,000-year-old mural that depicts a dog leading a blind person.

About Sam and his owner, Gill Lewis

I'm SAM, a Labrador retriever, just like Pip. We Labradors love nothing better than hanging out with humans, especially human puppies—they're always fun to be around!

I looked after GILL LEWIS's little ones. I was their faithful companion who traveled with them in cardboard rockets to the moon and sailed with them in a laundry basket across oceans to unknown lands. I listened to them read stories and tell me all their troubles. They were my very best friends, and I like to think I was their best friend too.

Collect all of the
PUPPY ACADEMY
stories!
PUPPY ACADEMY
SCOUT
and the Sausage Thief
Gill Lewis
PUPPY ACADEMY
STAR
on Stormy Mountain
Gill Lewis
PUPPY ACADEMY
PIP
and the Paw of Friendship
Gill Lewis
PUPPY ACADEMY
MURPHY
and the Great Surf Rescue
Gill Lewis
illustrations by Sarah Horne